☞ Porter is enjoying a season of rest, and show, his men are doubtless obliged to him for his kind consideration for their welfare. On Tuesday he fired a few shells from his parrots, and kept his men tolerably busy sharpshooting across the river, with no other result than might be expected. The mortars have not been used for nearly forty-eight hours. Poor fool, he might as well give up the vain aspiration he entertains of capturing our city or ex-termination our people, and return to his master to receive the reward such a gasconading dolt will meet at the hands of the unappreciating Government at Washington.

DEATH OF LIEUT.-COL. GRIFFIN.—General Smith's impetuous division seems singularly unfortunate. He has lost many gallant men whose valor and worth the siege has fully developed, and whose death is a great public calamity. Lieut.-Col. Griffin, commanding the 31st Louisiana regiment, was killed on Saturday. He was a popular and efficient officer. Gifted by nature with undaunted courage, indomitable resolution and energy, he was also possessed of quick determination, keen glance and coolness in danger, which are the most essential qualities of an officer, while by his mingled firmness and clemency of his conduct, he won the confidence and good will of his men. May the soft south winds murmur sweet requiems o'er his manes, and the twilight dews fall gently like an angel's tear-drop and moisten his turfy bed.

☞ If aught would appeal to the heart of the extortioner with success, the presstone of our citizens would do so. It ... to attempt to disguise from the ... own people that our wants are great, ... we can conscientiously assert our be... there is plenty within our lines, by ... re of prudence, to last until long after ... We are satisfied there are ... persons within our city who have ... ... secreted, and are doing it out, at ... exorbitant figures, to those who had ... foresight or means at their command to ...

Today Maryland is ours, to-morrow Pennsylvania will be, and the next day Ohio—now midway, like Mahommed's coffin—will fall.

Success and glory to our arms! God and right are with us.

☞ We have heretofore refrained from alluding to a matter which has been a source of extreme annoyance and loss to our citizens. We refer to the lax discipline of some of our company officers in allowing their men to prowl around, day and night, and purloin fruit, vegetables, chickens, etc., from our denizens, and, in the majority of cases, from those whose chief subsistence is derived therefrom. This charge is not confined solely to those at the works, but is equally, if not mainly, attributable to the wagoners and others in charge of animals. Several cases have come to our knowledge wherein the offenders have, in open daylight, entered premises, seized cattle and other things, and defied the owners to their teeth. We are pained to learn that an esteemed citizen of our Vicksburg, Wm. Porterfield, was under the necessity, in protecting his property, to wound one or two soldiers and deprive another of his life. We fully appreciate the fatigue, hardships and privation to which our men are subjected; but upon inquiry it may be ascertained that our city is second to none in contributing to the welfare of those gallant spirits who risk their life and limb for the achievement of an end which will make us one of the most honored people of the earth, and such conduct of which we complain is but base ingratitude. A soldier has his honor at much at stake as when a civilian; then let him preserve his good name and reputation with the same jealous care as before he entered his country's ranks. But so long as this end is lost sight of, so long may we expect to chronicle scenes of bloodshed among those of our own people. We make this public exposure, mortifying as it is to us, with the hope that a salutary improvement in matters will be made by our military authorities.

VICTIMIZED.—We learned of an instance wherein a "knight of the quill" and a "disciple of the black art," with malice in their hearts and vengeance in their eyes, ruthlessly put a period to the existence of a venerable feline that has for time, not within the recollection of the "oldest inhabitant," faithfully discharged the duties to be expected of him to the terror of sundry vermin in his neighborhood. Poor, defunct Thomas was well prepared, not for the grave, but the pot, and several friends invited to partake of a nice rabbit. As a matter of course, no one would wound the feelings of another, especially in these times, by refusing a cordial invitation to dinner, and the guests assisted in consuming the poor animal with a relish that did honor to their epicurean taste. The "cold" assure us the meat was delicious, and that pussy must look out for her safety.

☞ The Federal General McClernand is until recently outside the rear of our city has been superseded. He and Grant could not run in the same harness. The boys are deserting daily and Grant for gassing, both got the loggerheads. So poor Mac had to leave, and Grant has all his own way.

☞ The Yanks outside our city are considerably on the sick list. Fever, dysentry and disgust are their companions, and Grant is their master. The boys are deserting daily and are crossing the river in the region of Warrenton, cursing Grant and abolitionists generally. The boys are down upon the earth delving, the burrowing, the bad water, and the hot weather.

GOES OFF.—The National Intelligencer of Washington has closed its long career in a suspension and a sale of its effects at auction.— It has been highly respectable and very mileachievable in its day and generation. An old union prop falls with it. If we had, the writings of its epitath we should say, "Old Grimes is 'dead'."

NOTE.

JULY 4th, 1863.

Two days bring about great change. The banner of the Union floats over Vicksburg. Gen. Grant has "caught the rabbit," he has dined in Vicksburg, and he did bring his dinner with him. The "Citizen" lives to see it. For the last time it appears on "Wall-paper." No more will it eulogize the luxury of mule meat and fricasseed kitten—urge Southern warriors to such diet never-more. This is the last wallpaper edition, and it, excepting this note, from the types as we found them. It will be valuable hereafter as a curiosity.

LUCY'S CAVE

A Story of Vicksburg, 1863

Karen Winnick (signature)

Karen B. Winnick

BOYDS MILLS PRESS

HONESDALE, PENNSYLVANIA

For my family

Text and illustrations copyright © 2008 by Karen B. Winnick
All rights reserved

Boyds Mills Press, Inc.
815 Church Street
Honesdale, Pennsylvania 18431
Printed in China

CIP data is available

First edition
The text of this book is set in 13-point Stone Serif.
The illustrations are done in oils.

Endsheets reprinted with permission of Thomas Publications, Gettysburg, Pennsylvania

10 9 8 7 6 5 4 3 2 1

Boom!
Roar!

The house shook, and the windows rattled. Lucy covered her ears. "I hate the Yankees!"

Soldiers of the Union army were attacking Vicksburg. Their cannons thundered.

Lucy looked out the window and shuddered at the dark shapes of their gunboats on the Mississippi River.

"Hurry, Lucy," Mama called. "Papa's waiting."

Lucy pulled a shawl from the bureau and grabbed her favorite book and sampler and stuck them in her valise. She kissed her doll Higgity and put her inside, too.

The guns stopped. It was strangely silent.

Lucy picked up her valise and went outside with Mama, heading north toward the hills.

They passed houses half-standing, torn apart by cannonballs. Trees lay on their sides. Lucy's boots crunched over shattered glass.

Ahead was their church, and beside it the Reverend Lord's house, both deserted and covered with soot and ash. *Had he gone somewhere safe with his wife and son, Will, and his pesky daughter, Liddy?*

"Look!" Lucy pointed to the broken windows and piles of crumbled bricks. "My school is ruined!"

Street after street was deserted. Stores were shut tight. A stray dog wandered through the rubble, sniffing.

"No one would recognize our city," Mama said.

A few Confederate soldiers, their gray uniforms in tatters, straggled toward them. "Something to eat, please," they begged.

Lucy feared for her two older brothers off fighting. *Were they begging for food, too?*

A horse and wagon clattered by. Inside sat Lucy's classmate Sallie and her family.

"We're leaving town," Sallie called.

"We're going to the caves," Lucy called back.

Shells burst through the air.

"Down!" Mama screamed.

Lucy crouched behind a tree stump. She could feel her heart thumping like a drum.

Boom!

The shells exploded.

As soon as they stopped, Lucy scrambled to her feet, gripping her valise.

"Lucy, run fast." Mama pointed toward the hills. "Over there."

Caves dug out by the townsmen blotted the hills and ridges, glaring at Lucy like many black eyes. She hurried after Mama.

Cannons roared, louder than before. "They're so close!" Lucy cried. "Mama!"

Mama grasped Lucy and pulled her forward. "Hurry, hurry."

Lucy stepped over tangled roots and rocks. Her arms ached. She dropped her valise, then thought of poor Higgity inside. She picked it up and trudged on.

"Keep going, Lucy," Mama called.

Lucy moved closer and closer, panting as she stumbled over the last rugged part. Could she make it?

The muscles in her legs throbbed. She caught her breath and spotted the entrance beneath a clump of vines. Voices cried, "In here! In here!" Hands reached out. They pulled her inside and grabbed her valise.

Inside the dark cave, Lucy heard babies squalling and people coughing. She wrinkled her nose at the strong smell of sweat.

Lucy blinked, trying to adjust to the dimness. Sheets hung all over, and candles glimmered. There were so many people! She saw men playing cards. One man whittled a piece of wood; another strummed a guitar. Women and their servants sat close to the candles, sewing. Small children ran past, almost knocking Lucy over.

Strong arms suddenly lifted her off the ground.
Lucy knew those arms. "Papa! Papa!" Her head grazed
the ceiling. Then Papa kissed her and set her down.

"I've readied things for you," Papa said. "Follow me."
He led Mama and Lucy down a passageway. Flickering candles
cast eerie shadows all around.

"This cave has tunnels," Papa explained as they followed
him farther along.

Finally, he stopped. An old bed sheet hung from wooden
pegs hammered into the wall where the dirt was hard. Papa
pushed it aside. "This is our space."

Lucy stared at the space. She held out her arms and touched both sides of the wall. The length and width was not even as big as her bedroom back home. *How could they all fit?*

"There's no room to move." She set a blanket and pillow over a piece of carpet and some hickory planks that Papa had put down.

Someone pushed back the curtain. *Oh no!* Lucy winced. It was that bothersome Liddy Lord. She was living here, too!

Her brother, Will, and Reverend and Mrs. Lord greeted Lucy's parents.

Liddy pointed at Higgity. "Is that your doll? Does she have a name? Can I hold her?"

"You ask so many questions!" Lucy smoothed her doll's hair. "Her name is Higgity, and you can hold her for a little while."

Liddy hugged Higgity. "She's pretty."

"Be careful! You're crushing her dress." Lucy wondered how she'd be able to put up with Liddy's annoying ways.

"Lucy, come help me," Mama called.

Lucy snatched back Higgity. "Liddy, I need to go now."

A little later, when the explosions had stopped, Mama and Lucy waited their turn to cook outside over the common fire. A servant woman helped them lift the heavy iron kettle and put it over the flames.

Dinner was lumpy cornmeal gruel and rice. The sweet potato coffee gurgled in Lucy's stomach. The smell of cabbage from someone else's meal made her gag.

"I must leave," Papa said after dinner. "I'll be back every day to check on you." He gave Lucy a hug.

"Oh, Papa, I don't want you to go!"

"I need to go back and watch our house," he said. "Be careful, Lucy," he warned. "Never walk outside unless you're sure the guns have stopped."

The days passed slowly. In the evenings, Lucy read and stitched her sampler by candlelight.

Liddy often came and sat nearby. She peered over Lucy's shoulder. "What are you making?" she asked. "When is it going to be finished? What are you going to stitch next?"

There she goes again. Lucy sighed and yawned and went off to bed.

Many days and nights, the cave walls shook and rumbled from exploding shells. In her corner, Lucy clung to Higgity, worrying. *Is Papa safe? Is our house still standing?*

One evening, the gulls were quiet. Lucy stepped outside to sit by the entrance to the cave.

The air hung heavy and moist and smelled of burning wood. Lucy swatted away mosquitoes. It felt good to be outside, away from all the smells and noises and people—especially Liddy.

A patch of moonlight fell across Lucy's feet. She heard a whinny and looked up. Tied to a nearby tree stood someone's pony. Lucy went over and rubbed his forehead. He pressed his dry nose against her hand.

"His name is Cupid," said Liddy.

Lucy spun around. "Why are you always following me?"

"I . . . I wasn't." Liddy looked down. "I wanted to come out, too."

Shells zoomed in the sky. They screeched as they rose higher.
"We'd better get back." Liddy tugged at Lucy's sleeve.
They started to run. The shells burst with loud cracks.
The sky lit up.
Lucy stopped. The exploding shells sparkled like bright stars.
Papa would be angry, but she could not keep from looking at them.
"Lucy, hurry inside!" Liddy cried from the cave's entrance.

All night long, shells exploded. Lucy huddled with Higgity against the wall, which felt damp and scratchy against her skin.

Would those Yankees ever stop firing their guns? Would they capture Vicksburg? Shudders rippled through Lucy. *What was going to happen?*

Every day when Papa arrived, Lucy sighed with relief. "I'm happy you're safe, Papa."

He always brought two buckets, one with fresh water. Lucy and Mama used some water for drinking, some for cooking, and some for washing themselves and their clothes. When Papa left, he took away a bucket of their waste.

One day Papa showed Lucy the newspaper. "Because there's no paper left, *The Daily Citizen* had to be printed on wallpaper."

Lucy read that Union troops had made three charges into Vicksburg. Three times Confederate forces had driven them back. "We're beating them!" said Lucy. "But why are all these names here?"

Papa answered somberly, "Those are our townsfolk and the Confederate soldiers who have been mortally wounded."

Lucy shivered. Her own brothers might be in danger at this very moment. "I pray they're safe," she whispered.

One day, to pass the time, Lucy and Mama tried to make bread out of meal made from cowpeas and water. "Before the war, this was animal feed," Mama said.

Liddy came by. "Can I help?" she asked.

Lucy sighed and turned away.

"Of course you can," Mama said.

They kneaded and kneaded, but it was not like real dough. When Lucy pushed her hair from her eyes, the sticky yellow mess stuck to her cheeks, forehead, and eyebrows.

Liddy laughed. "Look at you."

Lucy pointed to Liddy's face, covered with the same mess, and began laughing, too. "Look at *you*."

More weeks went by. Lucy's eyes felt strained from the darkness, her skin prickled from the damp.

"Can we go home soon?" she asked Papa one morning.

"It's not safe yet," he told her.

That evening Liddy visited Lucy's corner with her brother, Will. Liddy held up a candle and said, "Look at the wall."

"That's my shadow," Lucy said.

"Watch what I've learned to do."

Liddy gave the candle to Will and began carving in the soft clay with a knife. Lucy tried to see what she was doing.

"Stay still, Lucy," Liddy said. She carved some more and stood back. "Now you can look."

"It's a silhouette of me!" Lucy said.

Liddy smiled and said, "You'll be here forever."

"I don't want to be here forever!"

Liddy's eyes filled with tears. She pushed aside the curtain and hurried out.

"I didn't mean to make her cry," Lucy mumbled.

Early one morning, when most people were still asleep, Lucy saw Reverend Lord leave the cave. Later, the church bell rang and rang.

It was Sunday! After all these weeks, Lucy had forgotten the day of the week.

When the guns were silent, Lucy thought it would be safe to go outside. She went off with Higgity to the hilltop and sat on the dew-covered ground. The sun warmed her shoulders. She closed her eyes.

In the distance, shots rang out. *They are far off*, Lucy thought.

Soon afterward, Lucy saw Reverend Lord hobbling up
the hill, a cloth wrapped around his leg.
   "Are you hurt?" Lucy called. "Do you need help?"
Shells whistled and hissed in the sky.
   "Get back to the cave!" Reverend Lord shouted.
Trembling, Lucy clutched Higgity and ran back inside.

A shell exploded. The ground shook and rumbled. A wall close to where Lucy was standing suddenly collapsed. She was knocked over. Earth and rocks crashed down.

I can't move. My legs and arms are stuck.

A mountain was pressing down on Lucy's chest. Her skin burned. Her nose and mouth filled with dirt. She coughed and choked and tried to spit out the dirt.

I can't breathe. Help! Someone help!

Lucy felt the weight begin to lift. She heard muffled voices.
Hurry! Please hurry!

A hand pushed dirt off her face. Someone wiped earth from her nose and mouth. She could breathe.

"Lucy." It was Mama's voice. "Are you all right?"

Lucy tried to open her eyes. They stung.

"Can you see?" Mama asked.

"I can see you, Mama." Lucy blinked. She could just make out the shapes of Reverend Lord and Liddy taking away rubble.

"Don't worry, Lucy," Liddy said. "We're digging you out as fast as we can."

Reverend Lord lifted Lucy. Hobbling, he carried her to her bed. Liddy brushed dirt off Higgity and put her beside Lucy.

Lucy moaned. She hurt everywhere—her arms, her legs, her neck.

Mama checked to see if she had any broken bones. "Everything seems fine," she said.

All through the night, Mama pressed a cool wet rag to Lucy's face. Liddy dozed while she held Lucy's hand.

Mrs. Lord stopped by, and then many others whom Lucy barely knew—the man who strummed the guitar, the servant woman who had helped with the kettle, the man who whittled wood.

After a few days, Lucy stood. Her legs were stiff and ached. The next day, she took some steps. Whenever she stumbled, Liddy reached out and held her arm to steady her. Each day Lucy walked a little farther. Then one day, when it was quiet, they walked outside.

Cupid whinnied. "He's happy to see us," Lucy said.

She and Liddy took turns feeding him mulberry leaves.

A week later, the guns were silent.

When Papa arrived at the cave, he gathered everyone around. "Our city has surrendered. The Yankees under General Grant will be occupying Vicksburg. Still, we should be proud. We held out for forty-seven days." Papa paused. "I'm not sure what awaits us, but it's time for us all to go home."

"Home," Lucy repeated, then looked around. She'd been through so much with all these people she'd hardly known. *I will miss them. I will even miss Liddy.*

"Do you think you could come and stay with Higgity and me until your house is fixed?" she whispered in Liddy's ear.

"I hope so," Liddy whispered back.

Lucy took her hand. "I hope so, too."

Author's Note

In May 1863, the Union army began the siege of Vicksburg, Mississippi. Gunboats fired on the city from their positions on the Mississippi River. Many citizens, including eleven-year-old Lucy McRae and her family, fled to hide in caves dug out of the hills around the city.

Some of the caves were small, others large, holding as many as sixty-five people. Families from all different backgrounds, as well as their servants (almost all of whom were slaves), lived together in close quarters.

The siege lasted for forty-seven days. It ended on July 4, 1863, Independence Day. From the upper porch of her home, Lucy watched General Grant lead his army into Vicksburg.

After the war, both of Lucy's brothers returned home safely. Later, she married and moved to Lewisburg, West Virginia. After her husband died, she remarried. She had one daughter, also named Lucy.

On June 8, 1912, Lucy's remembrances were published in *Harper's Weekly* as "A Girl's Experience in the Siege of Vicksburg." Lucy wrote, "I do not think a child could have passed through what I did and have forgotten it."

Lucy died in 1930.

The brick house overlooking the Mississippi River that Lucy and her family returned to after the surrender still stands on Monroe Street in Vicksburg and is known as Planters Hall. For years it was the home of the Vicksburg Council of Garden Clubs. Today it is a private residence.

My story is fiction, based on Lucy's remembrances and those of others. Gordon Cotton, historian at the Old Court House Museum in Vicksburg, provided invaluable help by answering my questions and showing me around the city. For my illustrations, I painted with oils in the style of artists of the Civil War era.

THE DAILY CITIZEN.

J. M. SWORDS......Proprietor

VICKSBURG, MISS.

THURSDAY, JULY 2, 1863.

☞ Mrs. Cisco was instantly killed on Monday, on Jackson road. Mrs. Cisco's husband is now in Virginia, a member of Moody's artillery, and the death of such a loving, affectionate and dutiful wife will be a loss to him irreparable.

☞ We are indebted to Major Gillespie for a steak of Confederate beef *alias* meat. We have tried it, and can assure our friends that if it is rendered necessary, they need have no scruples at eating the meat. It is sweet, savory and tender, and so long as we have a mule left we are satisfied our soldiers will be content to subsist on it.

☞ Jerre Askew, one of our most esteemed merchant—citizens, was wounded at the works in the rear of our city a few days since, and breathed his last on Monday. Mr. Askew was a young man of strict integrity, great industry, and an honor to his family and friends. He was a member of Cowan's artillery, and by the strict discharge of his duties and his obliging disposition, won the confidence and esteem of his entire command. May the blow his family have sustained be mitigated by Him who doeth all things well.

☞ Grant's forces did a little firing on Tuesday afternoon, but the balance of that day was comparatively quiet. Yesterday morning they were very still, and continued so until early in the afternoon, when they sprung a mine on the left of our centre, and opened fire along the line for some distance. We have not been able to ascertain anything definitely as to our loss, but as our officers were on the lookout for this move of the enemy, the expectations of the Yankees were not realized by a great deal.

Good News.—In devoting a large portion of our space this morning to Federal intelligence, copied from the Memphis Bulletin of the 26th, it should be remembered that the news, in the original truth, is whitewashed by the Federal Provost Marshal, who desires to hood-wink the poor Northern white slaves. The former editors of the Bulletin being rather pro-southern men, were arrested for speaking the truth when truth was unwelcome to Yankeedom, and placed in the chain-gang working at Warrenton, where they now are. This paper at present is in charge of, and edited by a pink-nosed, slab-sided, toad-eating Yankee, who is a lineal descendant of Judas Iscariot and a brother germain of the greatest Puritanical, sycophantic, howling scoundrel unhung—Parson Brownlow. Yet with such a character, this paper cannot cloak the fact that Gen. Rob't. E. Lee has given Hooker, Milroy & Co. one of the beet and soundest whippings on record, and that the "glorious Union" is now exceedingly weak in the knees.

Gen. Rob't E. Lee Again.

Again we have reliable news from the gallant corps of Gen. Lee in Virginia. Elated with success, encouraged by a series of brilliant victories, marching to and crossing the Rappahannock, defeating Hooker's right wing and thence through the Shenandoah Valley, driving Milroy from Winchester and capturing 6000 of his men and a large amount of valuable stores of all descriptions, re-entering Maryland, holding Hagerstown, threatening Washington City, and within a few miles of Baltimore—onward and upward their war cry—our brave men under Lee are striking terror to the heart of all Yankeedom. Like the Scottish chieftain's braves, Lee's men are springing up from moor and brake, crag and dale, with flashing steel and sturdy arm, ready to do or die in the great cause of national independence, right and honor. To day the mongrel administration of Lincoln, like Japhet, are in search of a father—for their old Abe has departed for parts unknown. Terror reigns in their halls. Lee is to the left of them, the right of them, in front of them, and all around them; and daily do we expect to hear of his being down on them. Never were the French in Algeria more put out by the mobile raids of Ab Del Kader than are the Federals of Maryland, Washington City, Pennsylvania and Ohio by the mercurial movements of Lee's cavalry. Like Paddy's flea are they to the Federals—now they have got them and now they haven't. The omnipresence of our troops and their throwing dust in the eyes, or rather on the heels of the panic-stricken Federals in Maryland,

Yankee News From All Points.

PHILADELPHIA, June 21, 2:30 A. M.—The following is all the news of interest in the Washington Star:

Major Brazill, of the United States volunteers, received intelligence from Fayette county, Penn., this morning that the rebels in heavy force were advancing on Pittsburg via the National road leading from Cumberland across the Alleghany Mountain. Their pickets had reached Grantsville, Md., thirty-eight miles from Uniontown, Fayette county, Penn., on Wednesday evening last.

It is reported in Washington to-day that two members of Hooker's staff, were gobbled up by guerrillas last night, in the vicinity of Fairfax.

HARRISBURG, June 20.—Operations were commenced on our side to-day by a portion of a New York cavalry regiment, capturing twenty rebel prisoners at McConnellsburg, in Fulton county.

Col. Lawrence, with a portion of the 127th Pennsylvania regiment, (mounted) captured a squad of rebels who were marauding on this side of the river.

We hold Chambersburg and the citizens are arming and fortifying the city. Gen. Couch had ordered that the place be held.

The Fortifications opposite this city are finished, and are considered impregnable.

The rebels are known to be 8000 strong at Hagerstown and Williamsport.

The rebels hold the north bank of the Potomac river, from Cumberland to Harper's Ferry. Gen. Kelly drove them out of Cumberland, and when they left they, threatened to return and furnish themselves with horses and forage. The rebels have done an immense amount of damage.

It is thought Gen. Rhodes is opposite Williamsport with 20,000 men. The rebel Gen. Imboden is reported as advancing, but this is considered doubtful.

FREDERICK, MD., June 20.—The enemy's cavalry left Boonsboro last evening, after capturing a number of horses, and returned to Hagerstown yesterday.

It is thought Gen. Ewell has left Williamsport and gone to the main body of his command, stationed at Charlestown. Lee's army is not known to be within supporting distance of Ewell, and it is very probable that the force now in Maryland will not penetrate further north. The cavalry force numbers about twelve hundred, under Jenkins.

WASHINGTON, June 20.—The enemy are reported to have crossed at Williamsport. It is not believed that they will visit Frederick.

The enemy has nearly 6000 infantry this side of the Potomac, under General Rhodes. Two regiments of infantry and a squad of cavalry are at Sharpsburg, and the remainder are encamped between Williamsport and Hagerstown. No artillery has been sent over, nor have any troops crossed since yesterday morning.

WASHINGTON, June 22.—The Richmond Dispatch of the 21st contains the following: "Dispatches received yesterday from Savannah announce the capture by the enemy of the

tremity of the city. These will be defended by Union League men, who are being armed by Gen. Schenck. The Union men are confident that the rebels will not be so rash as to attempt a raid in that direction. The disloyal among us are evidently uneasy, and begin to realize that any hostile movement of the rebel army against Baltimore might result disastrously among themselves.

A Herald's special from Monocacy Station. Md. the 21st, says: About 4 o'clock P. M., Major Cole, of the 1st Maryland cavalry, made a gallant dash into Frederick, with forty men driving out the enemy, killing two and capturing one. No loss on our side. Our cavalry passed through the city, and immediately after about 1500 rebel cavalry re-occupied the town.

Rebel cavalry entered Frederick yesterday P. M., about 6 o'clock, and dashed furiously through the city, capturing nine of our men on duty at the signal station, and paroled the invalid soldiers, numbering about sixty, in the hospital. A number of horses were seized. Secession flags were displayed at the Central Hotel, and some citizens collected there to welcome the rebels. A majority of the population evinced no pleasure at the visit. The ladies were exceedingly expressive in their demonstrations of disgust, and showered words of sympathy upon our prisoners as they passed through the town. The party which entered the city did not number over twenty, and many of these seemed to be intoxicated, as they reeled in their saddles. Pickets were stationed on the outside of town. No one was allowed to leave until about midnight, when the cavalry all left, going toward Middletown. This morning they entered the city again, and established pickets in the outskirts. The telegraph poles were cut down and the wires destroyed. There was supposed to be about thirty rebels in the city this P. M. The enemy has no force between Frederick and Boonsboro except a small cavalry camp at Middletown. No attempt had been made to destroy the bridge over the Monocacy river, although the enemy came down last night within a few rods of the junction.

The rebels are reported to be fortifying South Mountain. They have in the vicinity of Williamsport about 6000 infantry, 1000 cavalry, and a few pieces of artillery. A squadron of cavalry could undoubtedly capture the entire force this side of South Mountain.

Mid the din and clash of arms, the screech of shells and whistle of bullets, which are a continual feature in the status of our beleaguered city, incidents of happiness often arise to vary in a cheery way the Phases of so stern a scene. On the evening of the 20th ult., with gaiety, mirth and good feeling, at a prominent Hospital of this city, through the ministerial offices of a chaplain of a gallant regiment, Charles Royall, Prince Imperial of Ethiopia, of the Barberigo family, espoused, the lovely and accomplished Rosa Glass, Arch Duchess of Seaugamble, one of the most celebrated Princes of the Laundressia Regime. The affair was conducted with great magnificence,